This book belongs to:

eummdoig

Isla

All Ladybird books are available at most bookshops,
supermarkets and newsagents, or can be ordered direct from:

Ladybird Postal Sales
PO Box 133 Paignton TQ3 2YP England
Telephone: (+44) 01803 554761
Fax: (+44) 01803 663394

A catalogue record for this book is available
from the British Library

Published by Ladybird Books Ltd
A subsidiary of the Penguin Group
A Pearson Company

© LADYBIRD BOOKS LTD MCMXCVIII

LADYBIRD and the device of a Ladybird are trademarks of
Ladybird Books Ltd Loughborough Leicestershire UK

The Enormous Turnip

illustrated by Stephen Holmes

Ladybird

The old woman

The old man

The enormous
turnip

4

The girl

The boy

The dog

5

The old man
planted some
turnip seeds.

The turnip seeds
grew and grew.

One turnip grew
enormous.

7

"I want that enormous turnip for my tea," said the old man.

He pulled and he pulled, but he couldn't pull it up.

9

The old man called to the old woman.

"Help me pull up this enormous turnip," he said.

11

They pulled and they pulled, but they couldn't pull it up.

The old woman
called to the boy.

"Help us pull up
this enormous
turnip," she said.

15

They pulled and they pulled, but they couldn't pull it up.

The boy called to the girl.

"Help us pull up this enormous turnip," he said.

They pulled and
they pulled, but
they couldn't pull
it up.

The girl called
to the dog.

"Help us pull up
this enormous
turnip," she said.

They pulled and
they pulled and
they pulled.

Up popped the
enormous turnip!

And they all had
turnip for tea.

Read It Yourself is a series of graded readers designed to give young children a confident and successful start to reading.

Level 1 is suitable for children who are making their first attempts at reading. The stories are told in a very simple way using a small number of frequently repeated words. The sentences on each page are closely supported by pictures to help with reading, and to offer lively details to talk about.

About this book

The pictures in this book are designed to encourage children to talk about the story and predict what might happen next.

The opening page shows a detailed scene which introduces the main characters and vocabulary appearing in the story.

After a discussion of the pictures, children can listen to an adult read the story or attempt to read it themselves. Unknown words can be worked out by looking at the beginning letter *(what sound does this letter make?)*, and deciding which word would make sense.

Beginner readers need plenty of encouragement.